PUBLISHED BY PETER HADDOCK LTD.
BRIDLINGTON ENGLAND
© PETER HADDOCK LTD.
PRINTED IN RUSSIA

Contents

Little Red Riding Hood

Retold & Illustrated by John Patience

One day Red Riding Hood's mother baked a pie. "Put on your cloak and hood and go and see how Granny is," she said. "I fear she is not very well. Take this pie and give her a kiss. Make sure you go the long way round and don't take the short cut through the wood!"

So Red Riding Hood set off for her grandmother's house. But when she came to the wood she forgot her mother's warning and took the short cut. She had not gone far when she met a woodcutter. "Take care," he said gravely. "The wood is a very dangerous place for a little girl. Keep to the path and hurry on your way."

Well, Red Riding Hood took no notice of what the woodcutter had told her. She dilly dallied along the way and stopped to pick a bunch of wild flowers for her granny.

Alas, a big bad wolf was prowling around looking for his lunch and spied Red Riding Hood amongst the flowers. He had a mind to eat her up there and then but he could hear the sound of the woodcutter's axe and knew he must be working close by, so the wolf dared not show himself.

The wolf ran on ahead and waited for Red Riding Hood further along the path. "Good morning," he said politely, walking alongside the little girl. "Where are you going this fine morning?" "I'm going to see my granny," said Red Riding Hood. "She's not very well and I'm taking her a pie and these flowers." "And where does your old granny live?" asked the wolf. "At the far side of the wood," replied Red Riding Hood. "Well, I mustn't keep you," said the wolf. "Goodbye now." He watched Red Riding Hood out of sight then bounded off into the woods.

The wolf took the shortest way through the woods to Granny's cottage. He was already thinking about his next meal as he knocked on the door! "Who's there?" called Granny. "It's Little Red Riding Hood," replied the wolf, making his usually gruff voice sound very small and squeaky. "I've brought you a pie and some flowers, Grandma." Granny was in bed and not very well, so she cried, "Pull up the latch and come in."

The wolf pulled up the latch, went in, leapt upon the old lady and gobbled her up. Then he put on Granny's cap and spectacles and jumped into bed to wait for Red Riding Hood.

After a while, Little Red Riding Hood arrived and knocked on the cottage door. "Who's there?" asked the wolf, doing his best to make his voice sound like Granny's. "It's Little Red Riding Hood with a pie from Mother," came the reply. "Come in, dear," called the wolf. Red Riding Hood thought her Granny sounded rather strange, but she opened the door and stepped inside. She saw a figure in bed, wearing a nightcap and spectacles, with the sheets pulled up to the chin.

"Grandmamma, how strange you look today!" said Red Riding Hood. "What big eyes you have." "All the better to see you with, my dear," replied the wolf. "What big ears you have!" "All the better to hear you with, my dear," replied the wolf. "And, oh Grandmamma!" cried the little girl, "what great big teeth you have!" "All the better to eat you with!" growled the wolf. And, saying this, he leapt out of bed to grab Red Riding Hood! "Help!" screamed Red Riding Hood. "Help! Save me!"

At that moment the door was thrown open and in rushed the woodcutter. He had been passing by on his way home and had heard Red Riding Hood's scream. Whoosh! He swung his great axe and chopped off the wicked wolf's head. And, good gracious me! Would you believe it – out popped Granny! The old lady was a little shaken by her adventure, but otherwise quite well, with not a scratch on her!

"Do you know?" said Granny. "What I could do with now is a nice cup of tea." So they all had tea and ate the delicious pie which Red Riding Hood's mother had baked.

Later, as it was growing dark, the woodcutter lifted Red Riding Hood on to his shoulders and carried her home through the woods. You can imagine how surprised her mother was to hear the story!

PUSS IN BOOTS

Retold & Illustrated by John Patience

There was once a miller who was very poor and when he died all that remained for his three sons were his mill, his donkey and his cat. The eldest son took the mill, the second the donkey and the youngest had nothing but the cat.

"My brothers have done well," said the youngest son to himself. "If they get together they can make a living with the mill and the donkey, but what is to become of me?" "Don't be sad, master," said the cat. "Just give me a sack and have a pair of boots made for me and you will soon see that you have a better bargain than either of your brothers."

The miller's son was very surprised to hear the cat talk. "A cat that can talk may be clever enough to do as he promises," he thought. So, with the little money he had, he bought a pair of beautiful leather boots and the cat put them on. "Well now, Puss in Boots, what are you going to do?" asked the young man. "Wait and see," replied the cat and he swung a sack over his shoulder and set out into the woods.

The cat hid himself by a rabbit warren and soon tricked a silly young bunny into his bag. Then off he went to the king's palace. Once there, he demanded to see the king and was escorted into the throne room. "Your Majesty," he said, "I have brought you a present from my master, the Marquis of Carrabas." This was the title he had invented for the miller's son.

When he saw that the king was pleased with the rabbit, Puss caught other small creatures, such as hares and partridges, and gave them to the king, pretending that they all came from the Marquis of Carrabas. Naturally, the king began to feel very friendly towards the strange nobleman.

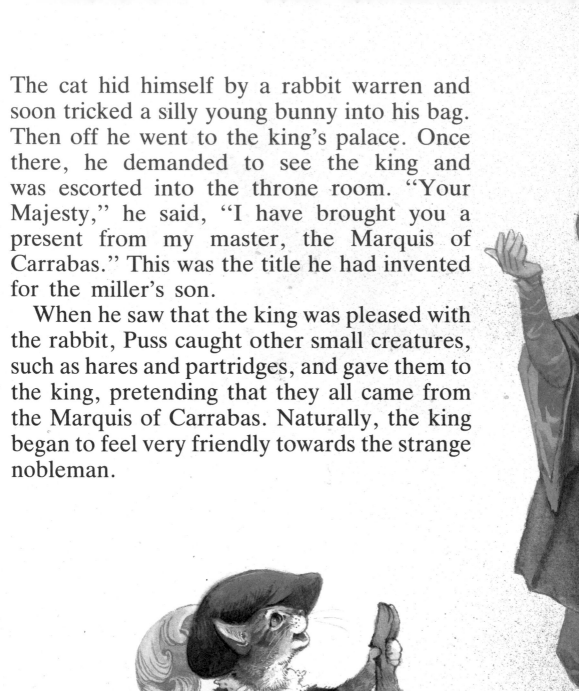

Now one fine day the cat heard that the king and his daughter, the most beautiful princess in the world, were going to take a drive by the riverside. So Puss went to his master and said, "You are in luck today. Just bathe here in the river and leave the rest to me!"

While the miller's son was bathing, the royal coach came by and the cat began to shout, "Help! Help! My master, the Marquis of Carrabas, is drowning!" Seeing that it was the cat who brought him gifts, the king ordered his royal guards to save the marquis. "Thank you, your Majesty," said Puss, "but what shall my poor master do now, for a thief has stolen his clothes?" The king was very sorry to hear this and at once offered the young man a suit of fine clothes. And when the miller's son was dressed in these rich clothes he looked every inch a marquis and the princess immediately fell in love with him.

The king then invited the miller's son to ride with them back to the palace, so the young man stepped into the carriage and sat beside the princess. Meanwhile the cat hurried on ahead. He stopped when he reached a meadow where a couple of mowers were working and he called out to them, "The king is coming this way. Tell him that this meadow belongs to the Marquis of Carrabas. Do this or I'll have you chopped up as fine as mincemeat!" The mowers were so frightened by the cat's fierce face that they did as they were told and Puss hurried on and ordered the reapers, ploughmen and woodcutters to do the same.

The king was amazed by the great lands owned by the Marquis of Carrabas!

Now the fields really belonged to an ogre who lived in a nearby castle. Puss knew about the ogre and called at the castle door.

"Sir," said the cat, "I have been
told that you are able to turn yourself into an elephant
or a lion." "Indeed, I can," said the ogre proudly.
And the next moment he transformed himself into a
great lion and let out a terrible roar which shook the
castle walls. The cat was so frightened that he
scrambled up on to the top of a high cupboard.

After a while, the ogre changed himself back into his own form and Puss jumped down again. "Well," said the cunning cat, "that was very fine. But I have also heard it said that you can take on the shape of a tiny creature, such as a mouse. I am sure that is quite impossible." "Impossible!" growled the ogre. "Why, nothing is impossible for me!" And in the blink of an eye, there was a fieldmouse scampering around the floor. With one leap the cat caught the mouse and gobbled him up. And that was the end of the ogre!

Meanwhile, the king had seen the castle and decided to pay a call on its owner. The coach rolled up to the castle door and waiting there was Puss in Boots. "Welcome to the castle of my master, the Marquis of Carrabas!" he called. The king was delighted to hear that his friend lived in such a splendid castle.

The young man invited the king and the princess into the great hall, where a feast had already been prepared by the ogre for his friends. Fortunately they did not arrive. When they had finished eating, the king declared that, since the marquis and the princess had obviously fallen in love, they ought to get married. This they did and lived happily ever after. As for Puss, he lived off the fat of the land until the end of his days!

Beauty & The Beast

Retold & Illustrated by John Patience

Once there was a rich merchant who had three daughters. Two were proud and lazy. The third and youngest was kind, considerate and hardworking.

Now it happened that the merchant lost all his money and the family was forced to move into a poky little cottage. The two eldest sisters did nothing but complain, but the youngest – who was called Beauty – looked after them all and comforted her poor father who was troubled by bills which he could not pay.

One day the merchant was offered work in a distant town. Filled with excitement he prepared for his journey. "Bring us back some fine dresses, hats and shoes!" cried the eldest sisters. "And what would you like, Beauty?" asked her father. "Come back safely and bring me a red rose," replied Beauty.

But the merchant's good luck did not last. It was mid-winter and, as he was passing through a deep forest, the snow began to fall. In the gloom he strayed from the pathway and became lost! Just as the merchant was giving up hope of ever seeing his family again, he saw through the swirling snow the lights of a great castle. He rode to the door and called out, but there was no answer. He stabled his horse and entered the castle. "Hello! Is anyone here?" he called, but he heard only the echo of his own voice. He found a table laid with food. He was very hungry so he ate but, though he saw no-one, he had the feeling that he was being watched. At last, tired out from his journey, he slept.

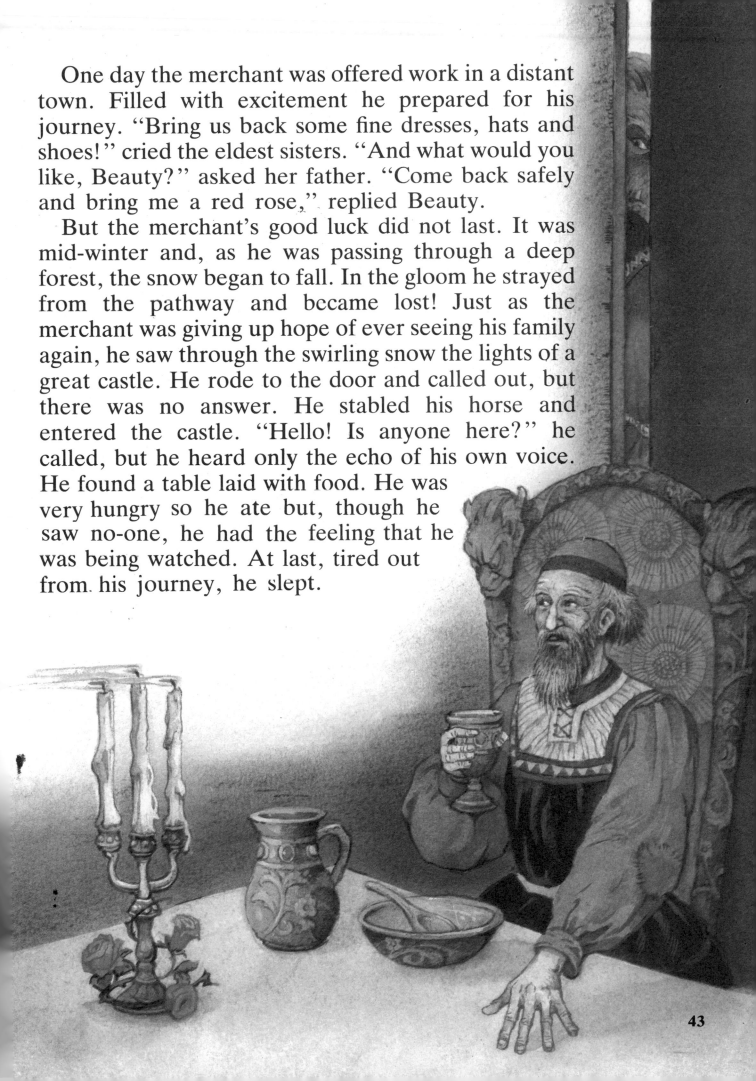

When the merchant woke the next morning he found a costume of fine clothes laid out for him. He ate a good breakfast and then went to the stable to find his horse. On his way he passed through the gardens. Though it was the middle of winter the flowers were all in bloom and not a leaf had fallen. Remembering his promise to Beauty, he stopped to pick a rose. At once there was a terrible noise. He turned and saw a monstrous beast. "Have I not given you enough, that you must steal the flowers from my garden?" roared the Beast. "I have a mind to kill you right now!" The merchant fell down on his knees and begged for mercy. "Your life will be spared," said the Beast, "if one of your daughters will offer to live with me here. Go now and let them choose. Do not try to cheat me or I will hunt you down and kill you!"

The merchant returned to his family with a heavy heart. He told them his story of the castle and the terrible Beast. Beauty could not bear to see her father so downcast. "Don't worry," she said softly. "I will go to live with the Beast. I am sure no harm will come to me." Naturally her father protested but Beauty insisted.

The following day the merchant and his daughter returned to the strange castle. The Beast was pleased. He gave Beauty fine dresses to wear and to the merchant he gave a chest of gold but he told him he must leave the castle and never return. Sadly, Beauty kissed her father goodbye.

So began Beauty's life in the castle. And as the days passed she grew fond of the Beast. Though he was frightening to look at, he was kind and gentle. In the evenings the Beast would play beautiful music and tell her stories of the strange lands through which he had travelled, while she sat by the fire and worked at her embroidery.

Still Beauty wished that one day a handsome young prince would come along to rescue her. Then one night she had a strange dream. An old woman appeared to her and said, "Do not judge by appearances. What is ugly on the outside may be beautiful inside." In the morning Beauty thought about the dream, but mistakenly she decided it was not important.

One misty morning the Beast found Beauty crying in the garden. "What is the matter?" he asked. "Your roses are beautiful," she replied, "but they remind me that if I had not asked my father to bring me back a rose I would not be your prisoner here." "Must you think of yourself as a prisoner? Don't you know that I love you? Will you marry me?" asked the Beast. "No, I cannot marry you," said Beauty. "You are so ugly." Then the Beast bowed his great head and wandered sadly away.

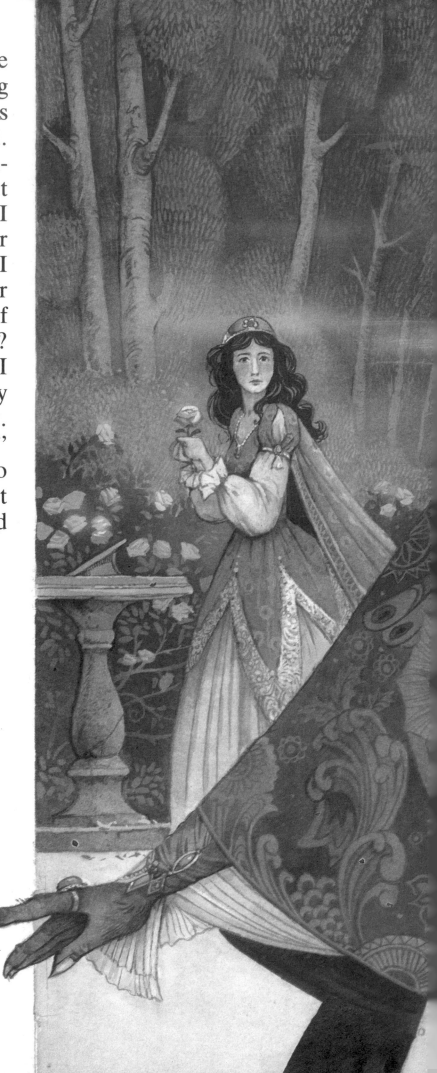

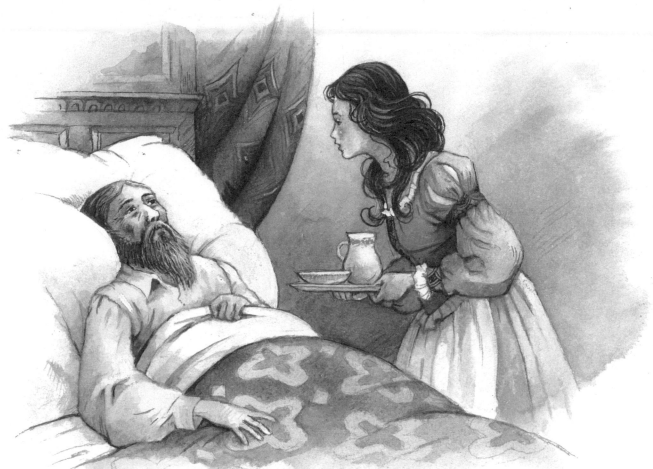

The next day Beauty found a mirror. She looked into it and there she saw her father lying ill. That evening she told the Beast what she had seen and begged to be allowed to visit her father. The Beast reluctantly agreed, providing that Beauty promised to return. So it was that the following morning Beauty left the castle. "Remember your poor Beast who loves you," cried the Beast, "and return within three weeks."

When Beauty arrived home her father was indeed very ill. However, as soon as she was there to care for him he quickly began to recover. The weeks passed by and Beauty forgot her promise to the Beast. Then one night she had a dream. She saw the Beast lying dying under a tree in the castle gardens and all around him the leaves were falling and the sky was as heavy as lead. Beauty awoke horrified! She rushed to her horse and rode like the wind to the castle. There she found the Beast lying dying, just as in her dream.

"Dear Beast," cried Beauty, "I did not realise before that I love you. Now I fear I have killed you." Beauty's tears fell upon the Beast's rough fur and slowly he began to revive. "Beauty, have you come back to me? Will you marry me now?" he whispered. "Yes, dear Beast," she replied.

Then there was a blaze of light, the Beast disappeared and in his place was a handsome prince. "I was bewitched," explained the prince, "by a spell that could only be broken when someone loved me in spite of my ugliness!"

Soon afterwards the prince and Beauty were married. Her father and her sisters came to the celebrations and they all lived happily ever after.

Pinocchio

Retold & Illustrated by John Patience

There was once an old wood carver named Geppetto who longed for a son to keep him company. One day Geppetto was carving a puppet. He had just finished making the head when suddenly it winked at him. Geppetto thought he must be imagining things and continued with his work. But as soon as he had finished the puppet's legs it jumped off the old man's lap and began to dance around on the floor. "You are alive, just like a real boy!" gasped Geppetto. "I will call you Pinocchio."

The old man was delighted with the puppet and made him some beautiful clothes. "You must go to school and learn to read and write," said Geppetto. "I'm afraid I can't go," replied Pinocchio. "I have no spelling book."

Geppetto was very sad because he had no money, so what did he do but sell his only coat so that he could buy his puppet son a spelling book. The next day Pinocchio set out for school, but on the way he passed a theatre. The ungrateful puppet forgot all about his father's sacrifice. He sold his spelling book to buy a ticket and went inside. Pinocchio was amazed. All the actors were puppets. "Hooray!" he cried. "They are my true brothers." And he jumped up onto the stage.

"Boo!" shouted the audience. "You are spoiling the show." But Pinocchio went on dancing with the other puppets. Soon the puppet master came to see what the trouble was. At first he was inclined to chop Pinocchio up and throw him on the fire, but the puppet pleaded so piteously for his life that he changed his mind. "Very well, I shall burn Harlequin instead," he growled. But Pinocchio was brave. "Do not burn Harlequin for he has done no wrong," he cried. "Burn me after all." These brave words touched the puppet master's heart. "I'll go without fire tonight," he exclaimed. "And you shall have a reward for your courage. Take these gold pieces and off you go."

Now Pinocchio honestly intended to buy his father a new coat and himself a new spelling book. However on the way home he met with a fox and a cat. The fox pretended to be lame and the cat pretended to be blind.

In fact the fox and the cat were a couple of rogues. They invited Pinocchio to share their supper. While he ate, the puppet told the villains all about the puppet master and his gold pieces.

Later the cat and the fox said goodbye and went on their way, but they hid themselves in the wood. They put on masks and hoods and as Pinocchio passed by they sprang upon him. Fortunately Pinocchio had time to hide the gold pieces in his mouth. When the fox and the cat failed to find the money they were angry. They tied up the puppet and left him dangling from a tree.

Now the blue fairy who lived in the woods flew to Pinocchio's rescue and took him to her home. "How did this happen?" she asked. Pinocchio began to tell her, but when he came to the part about the gold pieces he told a lie. He said the thieves had stolen them, but they were in his pocket. As soon as he told this lie, Pinocchio's nose grew two inches longer. He told another lie and his nose grew longer still and it went on growing until at last he could not get it through the door.

Then the blue fairy took pity on him. She called for some woodpeckers. They flew in through the window and pecked Pinocchio's nose back to its right length.

Pinocchio had learned his lesson. He promised never to tell another lie. He thanked the blue fairy for helping him and said goodbye. He knew that he ought to make his way back to his father. Instead he listened to a naughty boy who told him, "I know a place called Toyland where there is no school to go to, no rules to keep and lollipops grow on trees!"

At first Pinocchio had a wonderful time in Toyland. It was fun and games from morning till night. But all fun and no work was very bad for Pinocchio. He grew long, furry ears, a tail and hooves and he changed into a DONKEY! The wizard who ruled over Toyland sold Pinocchio to a circus and he was made to perform tricks to amuse the crowd.

One day, when Pinocchio was forced to jump through a big hoop, he stumbled and fell. This made him lame. He was no use to the circus now. The cruel ringmaster took him to a cliff and threw him down into the sea.

As soon as he was cast into the water the spell was broken and Pinocchio was changed back into a puppet. Alas, he was instantly swallowed up by a monstrous fish. Miraculously it was the same fish that had swallowed his father Geppetto when he had sailed out to search for Pinocchio. "My poor son!" cried Geppetto, hugging the puppet. "Now you too are a prisoner in this terrible place!"

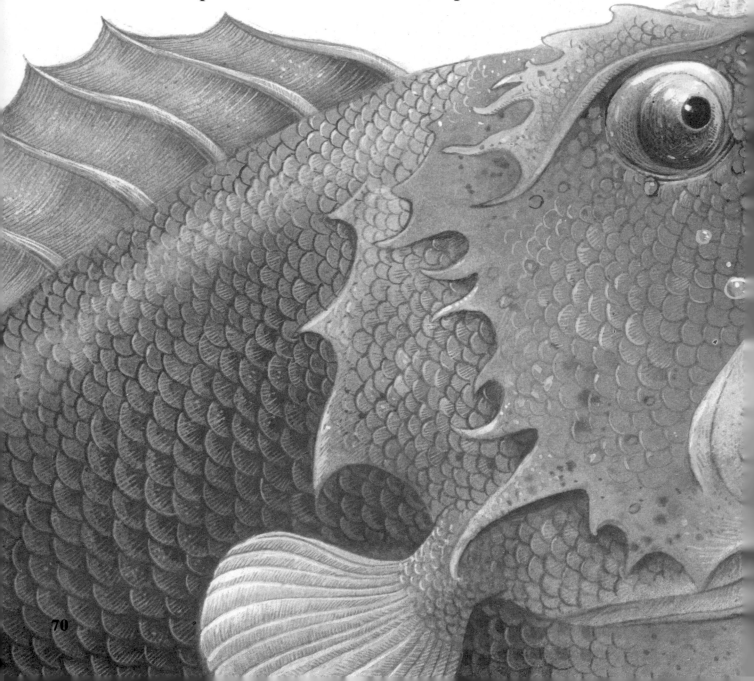

Pinocchio and Geppetto lived inside the giant fish for a long, long time. Then one day, quite suddenly, the monster gave a great sneeze. The wood carver and the puppet found themselves shooting forward, out through the fish's open mouth. They swam up to the surface of the sea. There they found a friendly dolphin who carried them both safely back to shore.

"I will never leave you again, Father," promised Pinocchio when they were home. As he spoke a strange light began to shimmer around the puppet and he was transformed into a real boy! It was the work of the blue fairy who had rewarded Pinocchio for his courage.

Geppetto was overjoyed. His dearest wish had come true!

CINDERELLA
Retold & Illustrated by John Patience

"Cinderella, scrub the floor." "Cinderella, make the beds." "Cinderella, why is my dinner not ready yet?" This sort of thing was all that poor Cinderella heard from her step sisters from morning to night.

Cinderella was very beautiful and good natured but her step sisters, who were very ugly, were uncontrollably jealous of her so they made her life miserable.

One day a messenger called at the house with an invitation to a Grand Ball which the Prince was holding at the Palace. At once the step sisters were in a dither about what to wear and how they should look. "All the most handsome young men in the kingdom will be there," they cried. "We must be sure to look our best!" "Oh please can I come to the ball?" begged Cinderella. The ugly sisters howled with laughter. "You go to the ball . . . don't be so ridiculous. Just look how tattered your clothes are. You can't go looking like that, and besides, we will need you to help us get ready."

Anyone but Cinderella would have refused to
help, but she was so kind hearted that she could not.
On the night of the ball the ugly sisters had Cinderella
running around in circles after them. "Powder my

wig . . . Press my gown . . . Do this up . . . Fetch me a mirror and do hurry up you lazy creature." Cinderella felt quite dizzy by the time they were finished and she didn't even get so much as a "thank you." Her step sisters swept out to their carriage and left poor Cinderella crying quietly by the fireside.

Suddenly there was a flash of light and, to Cinderella's astonishment, a little old lady appeared. "I am your fairy godmother," she said. "Dry your eyes. You shall go to the ball. Just do as I say." First she sent Cinderella to the garden to find a pumpkin. She touched it with her magic wand and in an instant it became the most splendid coach you ever saw.

Then Cinderella was told to bring the mouse trap from the kitchen. Inside it were six white mice. The fairy godmother gave each of them a tap with her wand and turned them into snow white horses.

Next, Cinderella brought six little lizards which she found in a watering can.

These were turned into six footmen with silver-buttoned coats.

Finally a large black rat was transformed into a jolly coachman.

"Well now, child — you can go to the ball after
all," chuckled the fairy godmother. "Aren't you
pleased?" "Oh yes," exclaimed Cinderella, "But
how can I go in these old rags?" At once the
godmother waved her wand and the dirty old clothes
were changed into a beautiful ball gown and around
Cinderella's neck was a string of pearls. Then, to

82

complete the picture, she found a pair of dainty glass slippers on her feet. "Now, off you go and enjoy yourself," said the fairy godmother. "But remember, you must not stay a second after midnight or all your fine clothes will turn back into rags and the coach and horses, coachman and footmen will return to what they were before I worked my magic."

Cinderella arrived at the palace just as the ball was about to begin. As she entered the ballroom a murmur ran around the crowd. "Who is that beautiful girl?" The Prince could not take his eyes off her. He insisted that she dance with him for the entire evening. Cinderella had never been so happy before in her entire life. She was so happy that she didn't notice the time flying by until, suddenly, the

clock began to strike twelve. "Good heavens!" she cried, remembering her fairy godmother's warning. "I must go." She ran out into the darkness. At the twelfth stroke her fine clothes became rags and the coach turned back into a pumpkin. The Prince ran after Cinderella but she had vanished into the night. All that remained was one of her glass slippers. It had fallen from her foot as she ran down the palace steps. "I will find the girl who wore this slipper," vowed the Prince. "And I will make her my bride."

The next morning a proclamation was read out in the square to the sound of a trumpet. Every girl in the kingdom was to try on the glass slipper and whoever it fitted would marry the Prince. From North and South, East and West, people came flocking to the city. Young and old, short and tall, thin and fat; one by one they tried on the glass slipper, but it fitted none of them.

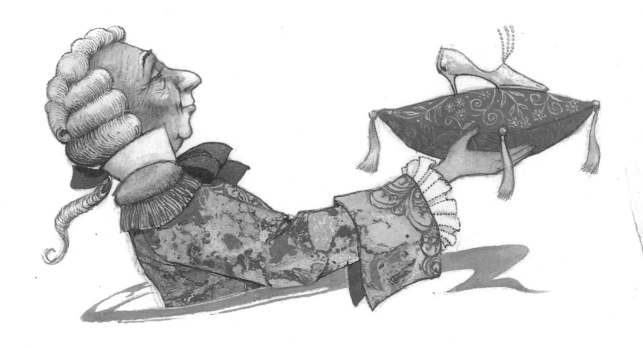

Eventually the slipper was brought to Cinderella's house. The ugly sisters were so excited. They snatched the glass slipper from the messenger before he could say a word. "Look! It fits me!" cried the elder sister. "Nonsense," said the younger sister. "Your heel is sticking out. Let me try it on. There it fits me like a glove." "Well, it certainly doesn't fit like a slipper!" sneered the elder one. "Your toes are bent double." "Does anyone else live here?" asked the messenger. "Everyone must try on the slipper." "Only Cinderella," replied the sisters. "But she's only a servant girl. The slipper can't possibly fit her." But the messenger insisted that even Cinderella must try on the slipper, and so she was brought from the kitchen where she had been cooking dinner. Slowly, she took the slipper and put it on. The ugly sisters gasped in amazement. "It fits," they wailed.

Then Cinderella's fairy godmother appeared and tapped her with the magic wand. Once more she was dressed in fine clothes, even more beautiful than her ball gown. "Your carriage is waiting to take you to the palace," said the fairy godmother. The Prince was overjoyed to see Cinderella again. Soon the couple were married. Everyone went to the wedding, even the ugly sisters whom Cinderella had completely forgiven for their previous unkindness.

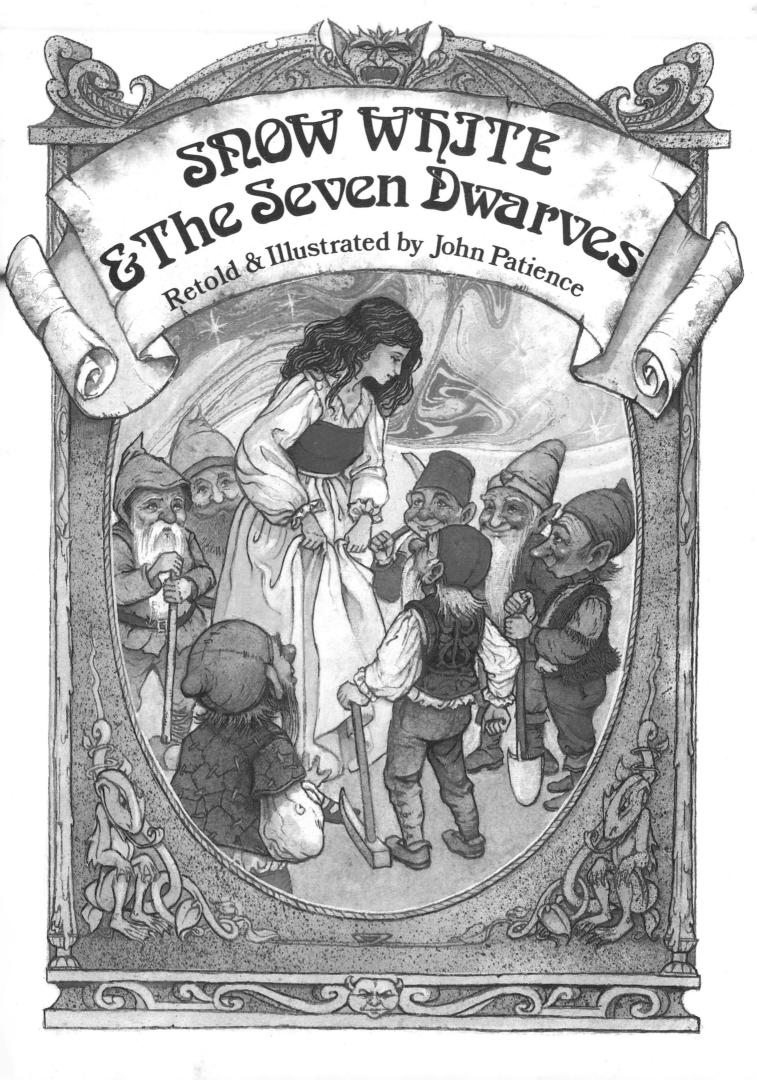

SNOW WHITE
& The Seven Dwarves

Retold & Illustrated by John Patience

Once upon a time a queen sat sewing by her window. Snow flakes were falling outside, and as she watched them settling on her black ebony windowsill, she pricked her finger with the needle and a drop of red blood fell onto the snow. Then she thought to herself, "I wish I had a daughter with skin as white as that snow, with cheeks as red as blood and hair as ebony black as the window frame."

Strangely, the queen's wish came true and she gave birth to a beautiful baby girl whom she named Snow White. But alas the queen died when Snow White was born and before long the king married again.

The new queen was very beautiful but she was evil and vain and could not bear to think that anyone might be lovelier than she. She had a magic mirror which she would look into every day, saying:

"Mirror, mirror on the wall,
Who is the fairest of them all?"
The mirror's answer was always the same:
"Thou art the fairest,"
until one fateful day, when Snow White had grown up, it replied:
"Thou art fair and beauteous to see,
But Snow White is fairer far than thee."

At these words the queen flew into a terrible rage. She called a servant and ordered him to take Snow White into the forest and kill her!

The servant knew he was meant to kill Snow White, but he couldn't do it, so he left her in the forest at the mercy of the weather and the wild beasts.

Soon Snow White began to feel frightened and hungry. She wandered around, looking for berries that she might eat. Suddenly she saw a tiny cottage. She went up to the door and knocked. There was no answer so she went inside. The room was cosy and warm and the table was laid for supper. A stew bubbled in the pot which hung over the fire. The smell was irresistible and Snow White helped herself to some. Then, feeling sleepy, she went upstairs and lay down on one of the seven little beds she found there.

Presently in came the owners of the cottage — seven little dwarfs who worked in the mountains digging for gold. They saw immediately that all was not right; there was a dirty plate on the table! They all crept up the stairs and then one of them whispered, "Look, someone is sleeping in my bed!" His brothers were filled with wonder and astonishment and came with their lamps to look at

Snow White. "Good heavens! What a lovely child she is," they whispered. The dwarfs were delighted to find her and took great care not to wake her, but fussed around as quietly as little mice, tucking her in and making her snug.

The next morning, Snow White told the dwarfs her story and they took pity on her. They decided to let her live in their cottage with them, and in return she could keep the place clean and cook their meals while they were out digging for gold. Snow White soon settled into her new home and was very happy because the dwarfs were much kinder to her than her stepmother had been.

It seemed that Snow White would live happily ever after with the seven dwarfs, until one day her stepmother looked into the magic mirror and asked it who was the fairest in the land.

"Queen, thou art of beauty rare,"
replied the mirror,
"But Snow White living in the glen,
With the seven little men,
Is a thousand times more fair."

When the queen realised that her servant had deceived her and Snow White was still alive, she was terribly angry. She locked herself in a secret room in the castle and brewed a horrible poison which she put into a beautiful, rosy, red apple. Then, disguised as a gipsy, the queen set out for the dwarfs' cottage.

The evil queen knocked on the cottage door and begged to be let in, but the dwarfs had warned Snow White not to open the door to strangers and so she refused. "Silly girl," said the queen, "I've brought you a lovely apple. Take it."

"Oh, what harm can it do?" thought Snow White. She opened the door and took a bite from the apple. Immediately she fell down dead upon the floor.

When the dwarfs found Snow White they were all heartbroken. They tried every way they could to revive her, but it was no good. At last they gave up hope and made her a beautiful crystal coffin, which they placed in a forest glade. Every day they brought fresh flowers and placed them around the coffin and wept for her.

One day a Prince came riding by. When he saw Snow White he fell in love with her and, opening her coffin, he lifted her in his arms. As he did so the piece of apple which the dwarfs didn't realise was lodged in her throat, fell from her mouth. She opened her eyes and fell in love with the prince at first sight.

The wicked queen could not believe it when her mirror said,

"Oh queen, although you are of beauty rare,

The Prince's bride is a thousand times more fair." She was so furious that she choked and died.

Now Snow White had nothing to fear from the wicked queen and she lived happily ever after with her prince in a fine palace, where they were often visited by seven dwarfs.

GOLDILOCKS
and
The Three Bears

Retold & Illustrated by John Patience

Once upon a time there was a little girl called Goldilocks who lived on the edge of a great forest. She was called Goldilocks because she had very beautiful curly blond hair which gleamed like gold in the sunlight. But although Goldilocks looked so pretty she could sometimes be very naughty. Every day as Goldilocks went out to play, her mother would remind her: "Now Goldilocks, you may go and play in the meadow, but don't go into the wood, or you will get lost."

One morning Goldilocks began to grow tired of playing on the swing in the meadow. She couldn't catch any minnows in the stream and even her favourite doll seemed boring. "I know," said Goldilocks to herself, "I'll go exploring in the forest!" She glanced back at the house to make sure her mother wasn't watching, then off she ran across the meadow and into the forest.

Goldilocks wandered deeper and deeper into the forest until, at last, she became completely lost. The trees began to appear menacing, she imagined she could see faces in them, peering down at her; and once she thought she heard a deep growling noise like the sound of a wild animal. She felt very frightened and was about to cry when, to her surprise, she saw a strange little cottage amongst the trees. It was thatched with fur! Goldilocks tapped on the door but there was no answer. Then she peeped in through an open window. There was no one home so Goldilocks climbed inside for a look around.

Inside the cottage a log fire was burning brightly and a table was laid for breakfast with three bowls of steaming porridge. It smelled delicious and Goldilocks suddenly realised how hungry she was. "I'll just try a little to see how it tastes," she said. First she tried the largest bowl, but it was too salty. Next she tried the middle-sized bowl, but it was too sweet. Finally she tried the little bowl. "That's just right," she cried and she ate it all up.

Round the fireside were three chairs. Feeling tired, Goldilocks decided to sit down. First she tried the big chair, but it was very uncomfortable. Next she tried the middle-sized chair, but that was no better. Then she tried the little chair, but it was too small and broke into pieces.

In the corner of the room was a staircase and Goldilocks climbed up to see what was at the top. There she found a bedroom with three beds in it — and of course, one was very big, one was middle-sized and one was small. She tried each bed in turn. The large one was too hard, the middle-sized one was too soft, but the little one was just right, and Goldilocks soon fell fast asleep.

Goldilocks would not have slept so peacefully if she had known that the cottage belonged to three bears, and at that moment they were coming down the woodland path on their way home. Father bear and baby bear had been collecting firewood, and mother bear had collected a basket full of blackberries. "I do hope the porridge you made for breakfast will be cool enough to eat now," said baby bear to his mother as the cottage came into view. "I am very hungry."

As soon as they got into the house, the three bears went to the table to eat up their porridge. "Somebody," growled father bear in his big gruff voice, "Somebody has been eating my porridge." "Somebody," said mother bear in her medium-sized voice, "Somebody has been eating my porridge too." "And somebody has been eating my porridge, and eaten it all up!" cried baby bear in his baby-sized voice.

Then father bear noticed that the pipe he had left on his chair had been brushed off onto the floor. "Who's been sitting in my chair?" he roared in his great big voice.

"Who's been sitting in my chair?" said mother bear in her medium-sized voice. "And who's been sitting in my chair and broken it all to pieces?" cried poor little baby bear in his tiny little voice.

"Look, someone has left muddy footprints," growled father bear. "They go all the way up the stairs."

As soon as they were inside the bedroom, father bear growled in his big gruff voice, "Somebody has been lying on my bed." "Somebody has been lying on my bed too," said mother bear in her medium-sized voice. "Somebody has been lying on my bed," cried baby bear," and they're still there, fast asleep!"

The three bears gathered around and stared in astonishment at the pretty little girl with golden curls. Who on earth was she? And what was she 124 doing in their cottage?

Goldilocks woke up with a start and rubbed her eyes. She thought that the three bears were part of her dream, so she pinched herself hard, but the bears did not disappear. Now she was very frightened. "Goodness me, you're real!" she cried and, jumping out of bed, she ran down the stairs and out through the front door. On and on she ran, not stopping for breath until at last she reached the edge of the forest and saw her own house, with her mother waiting on the doorstep for her. And she never went exploring in the forest again!

125